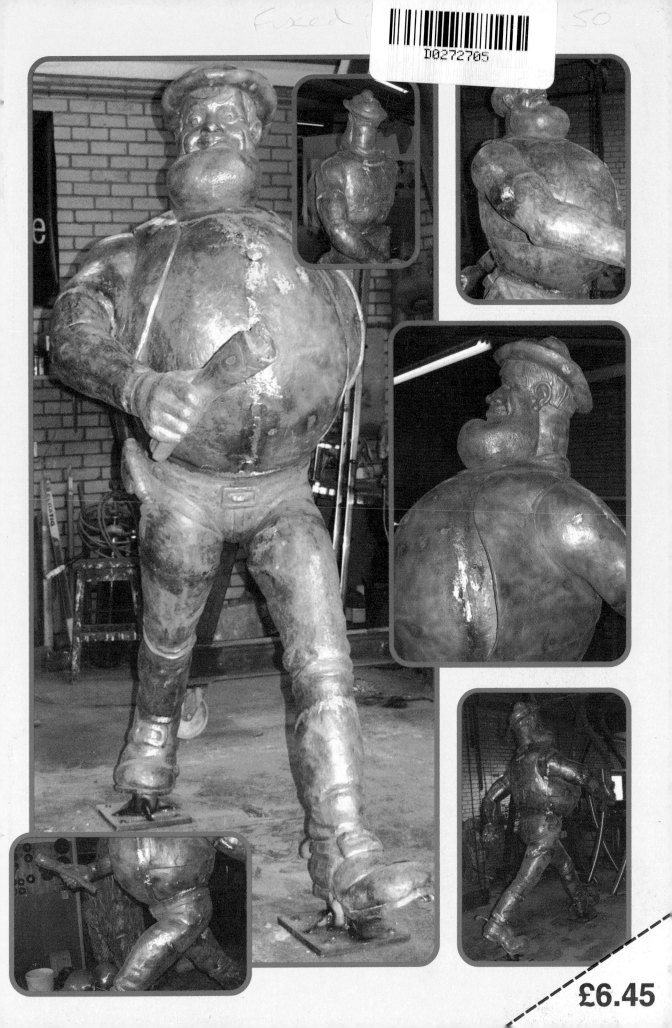

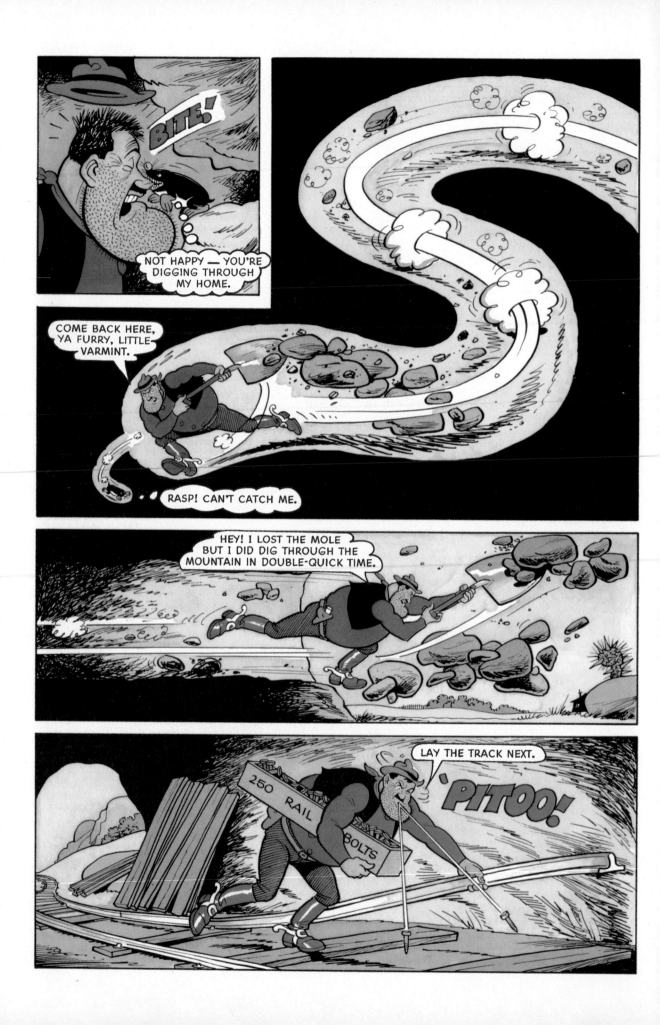

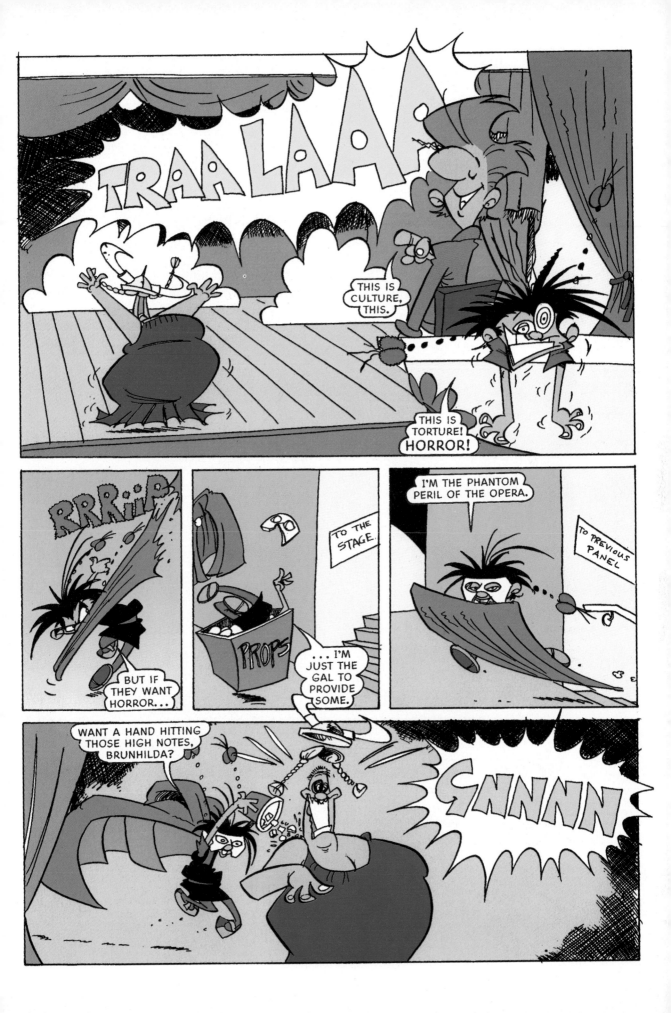

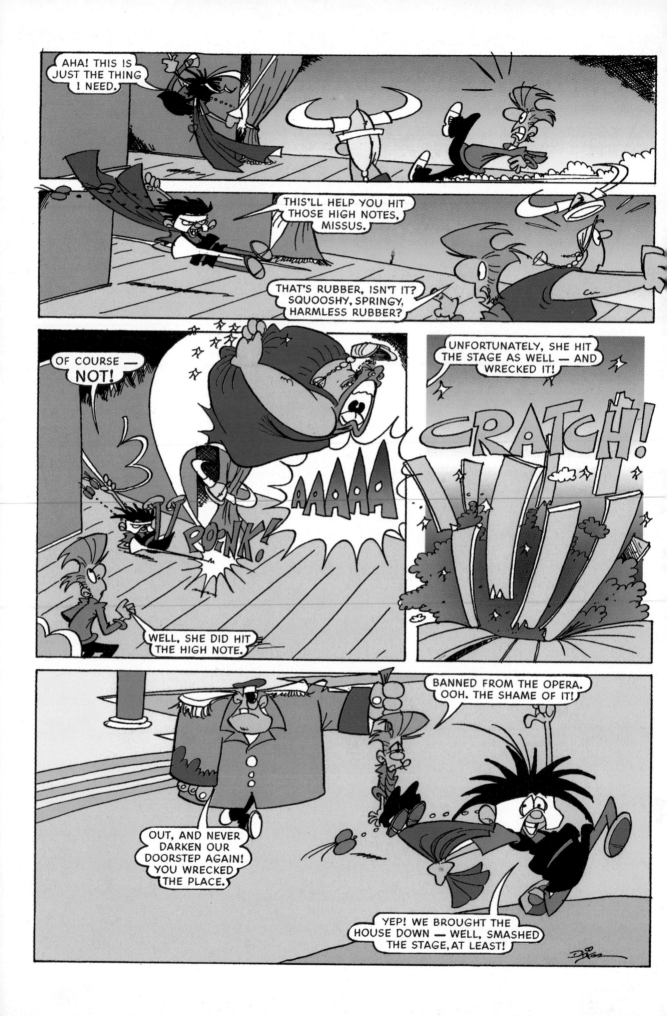

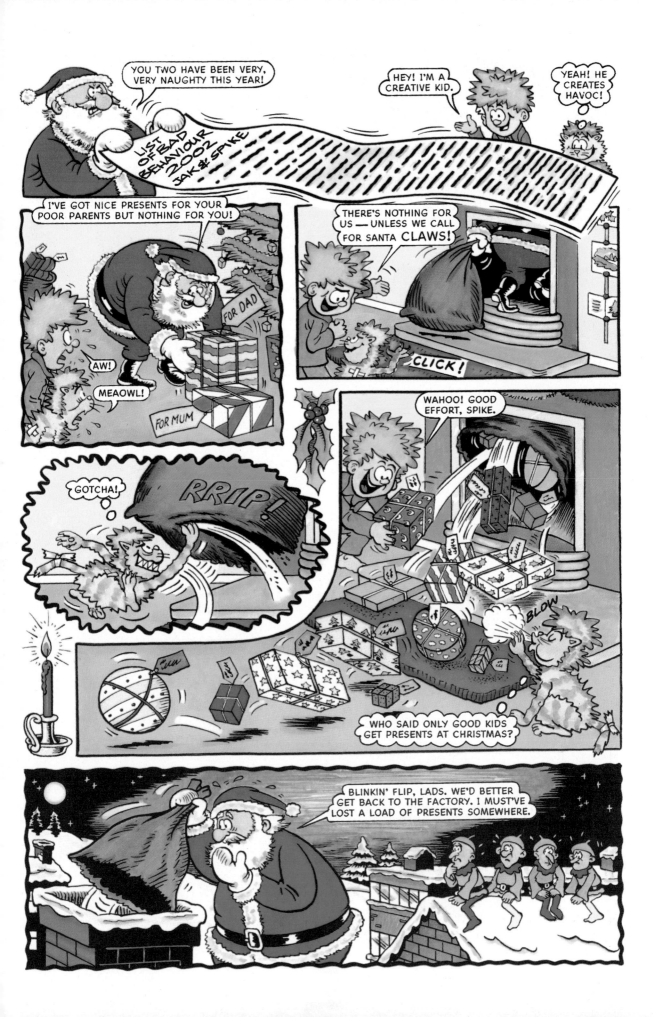

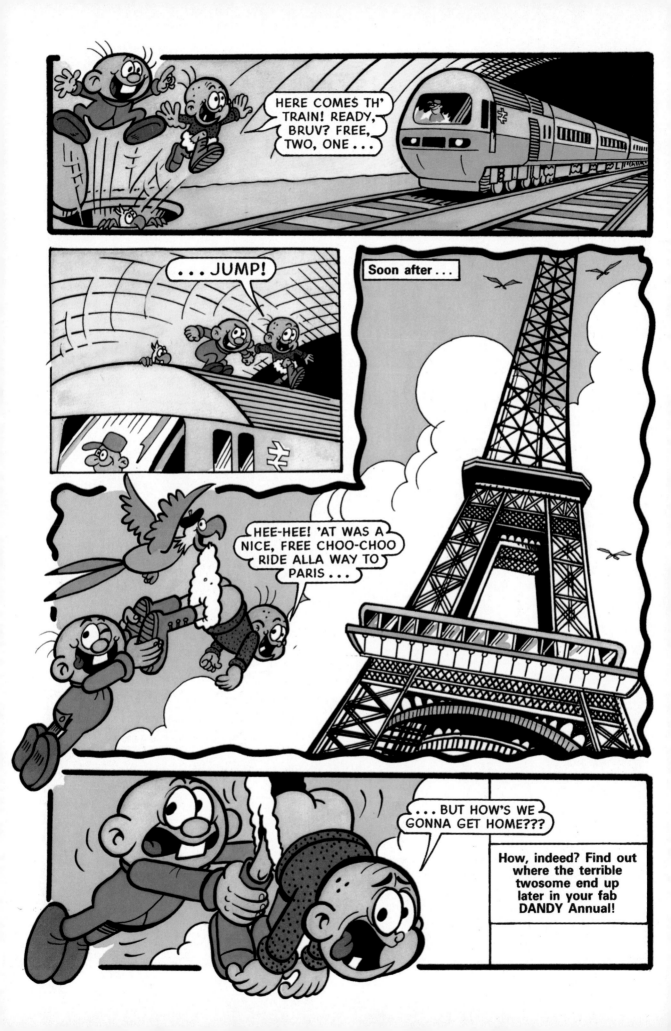

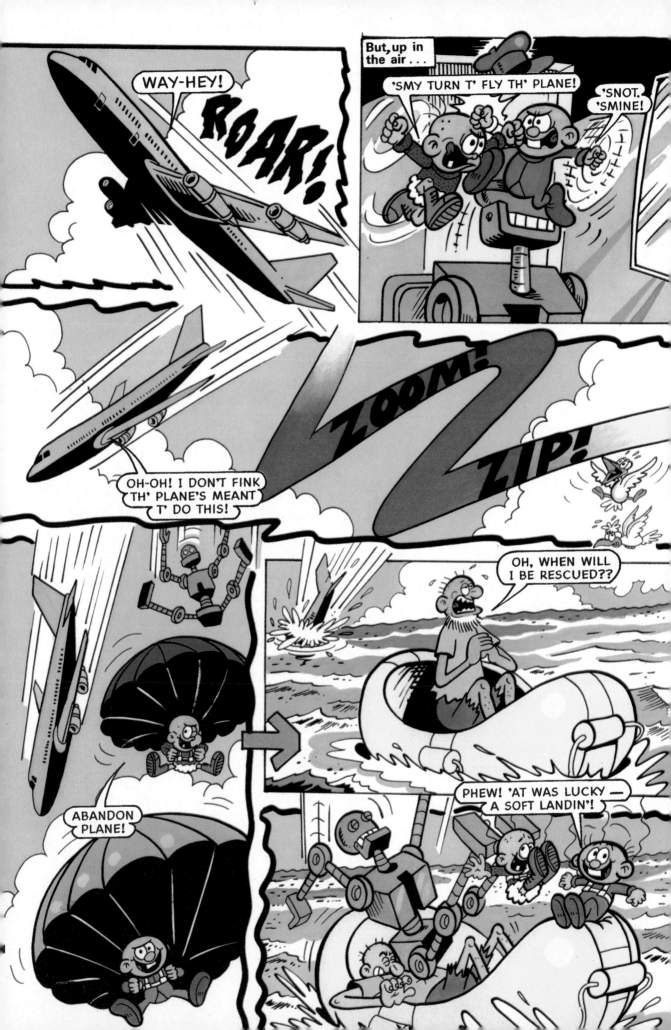

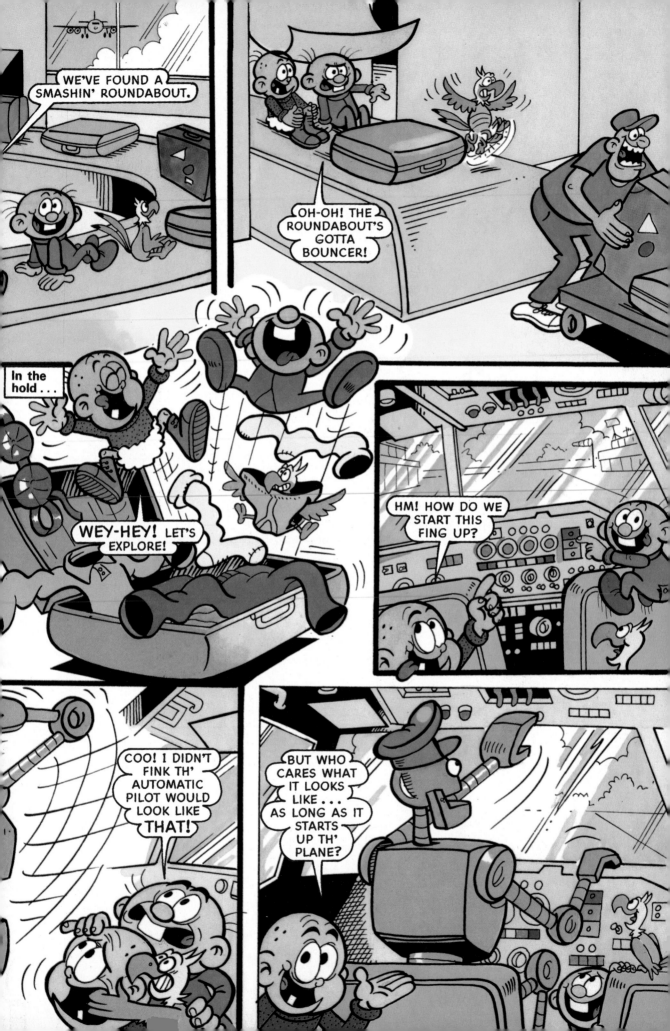

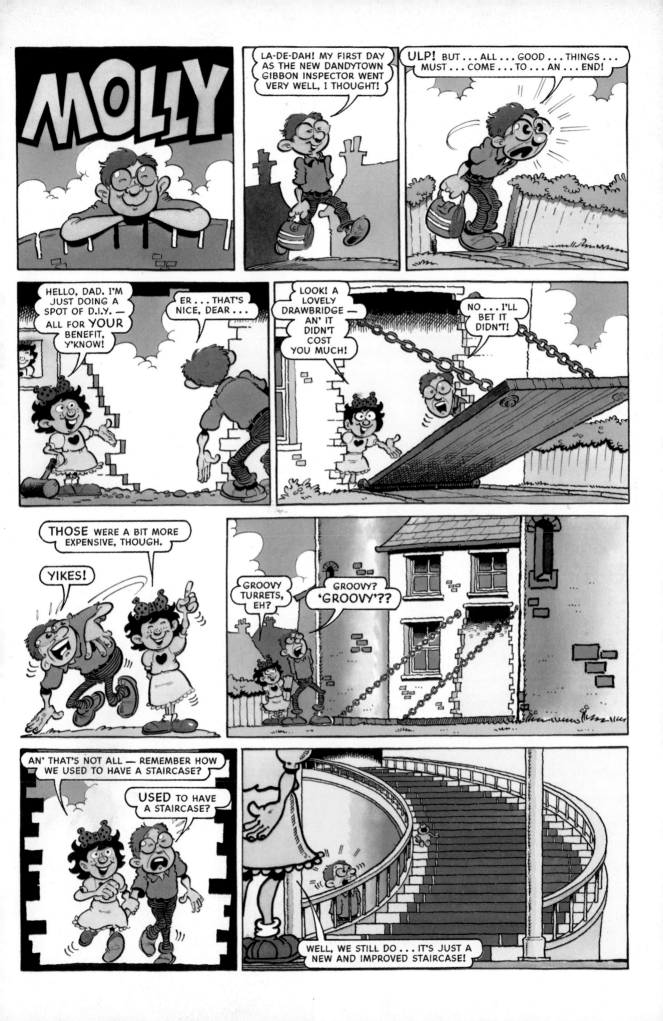

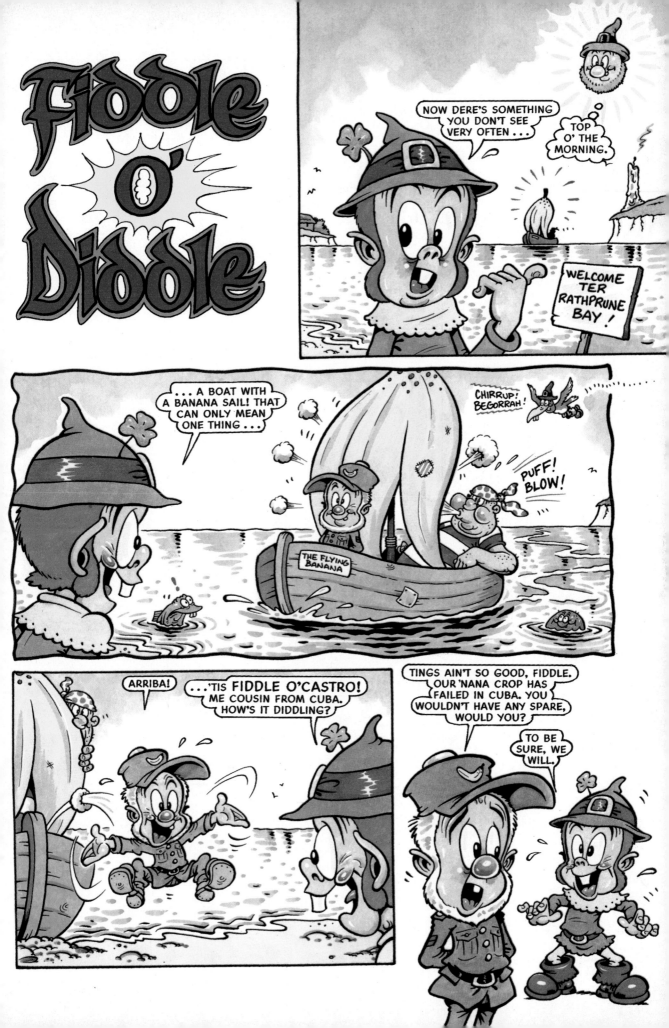

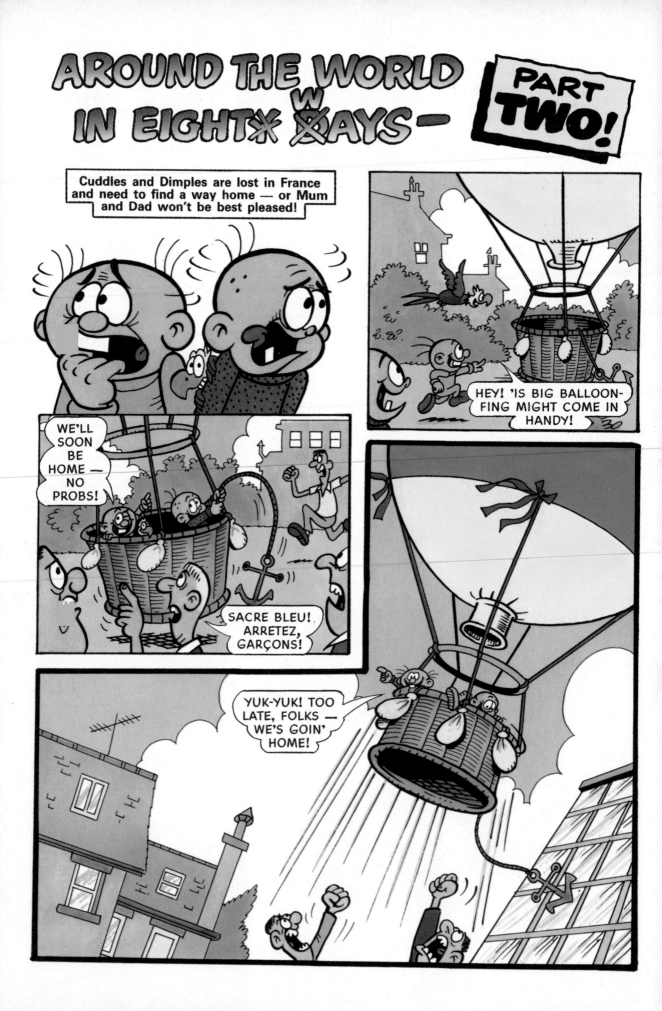

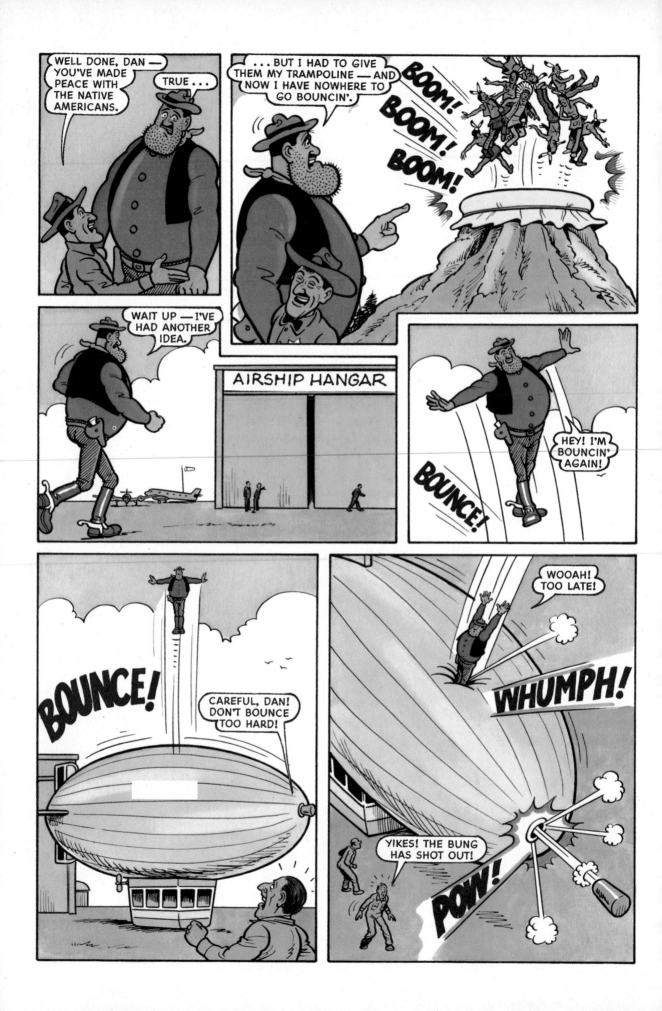

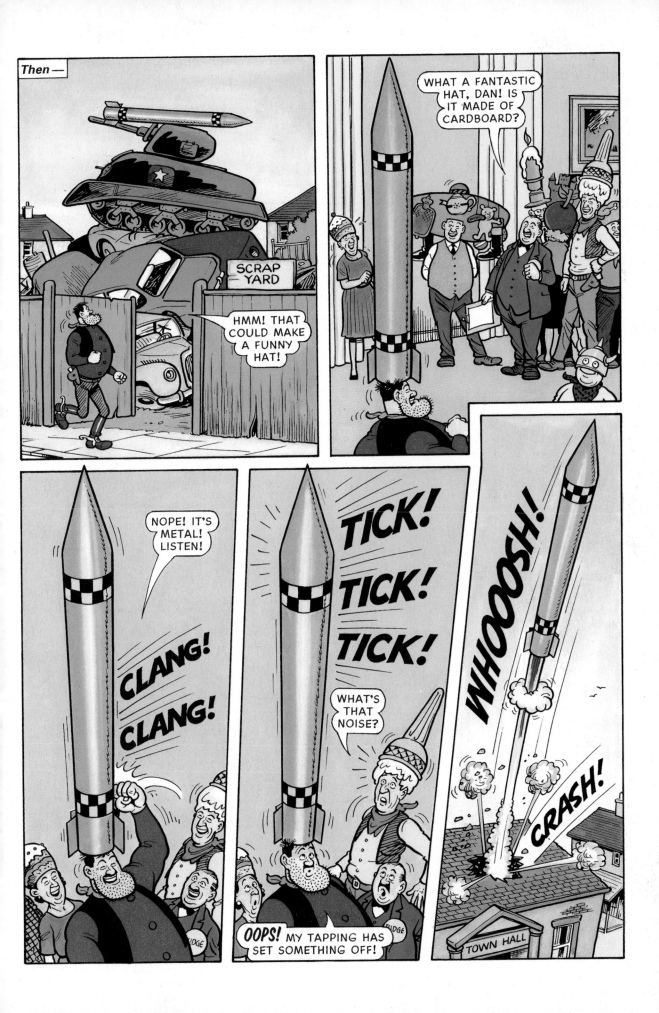

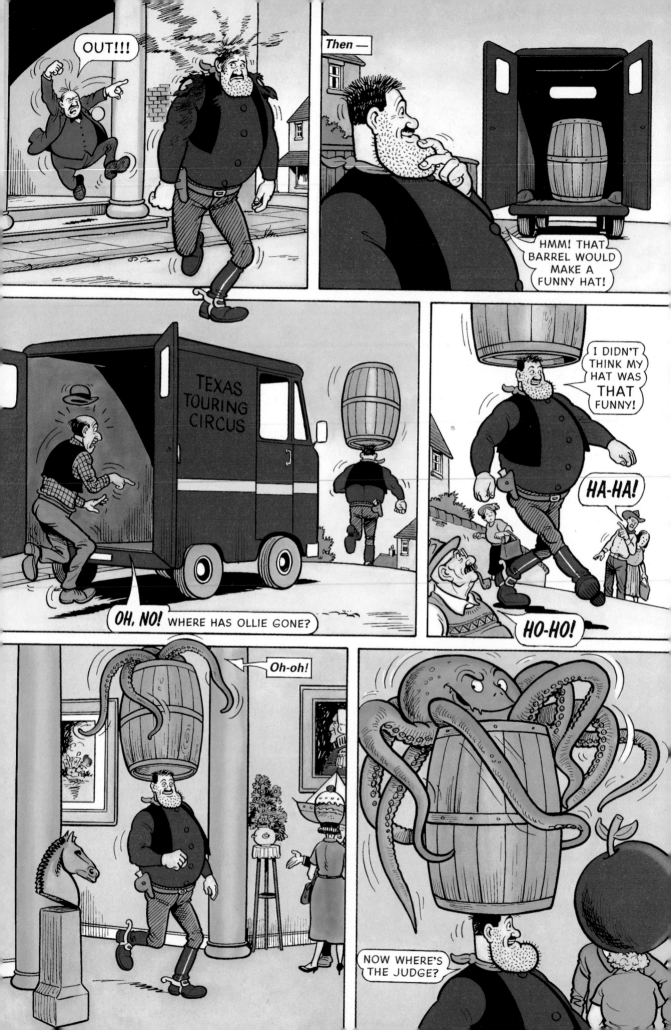

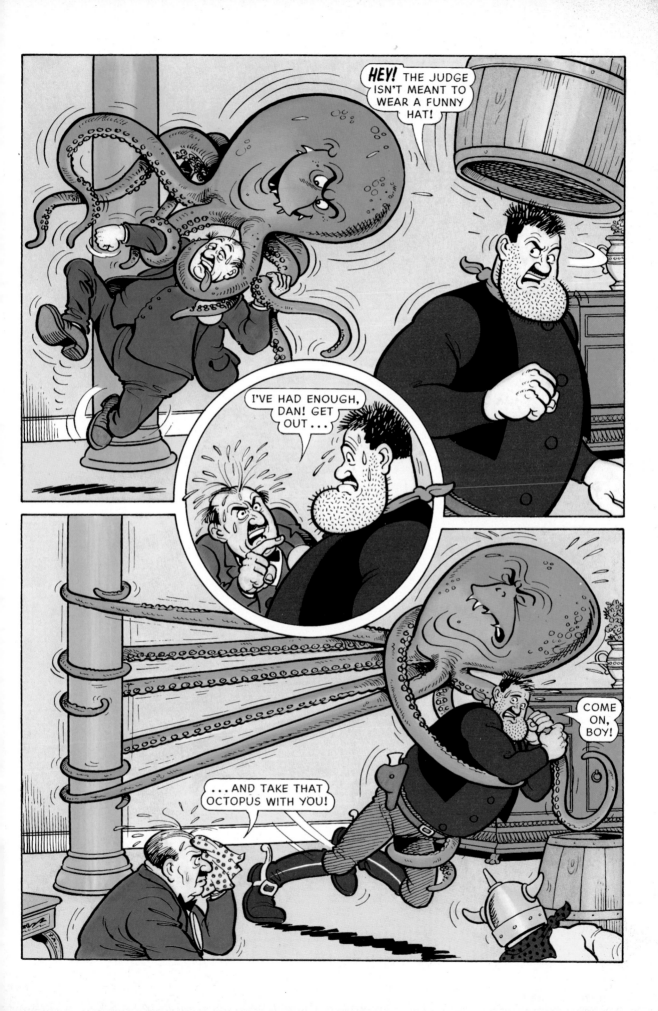

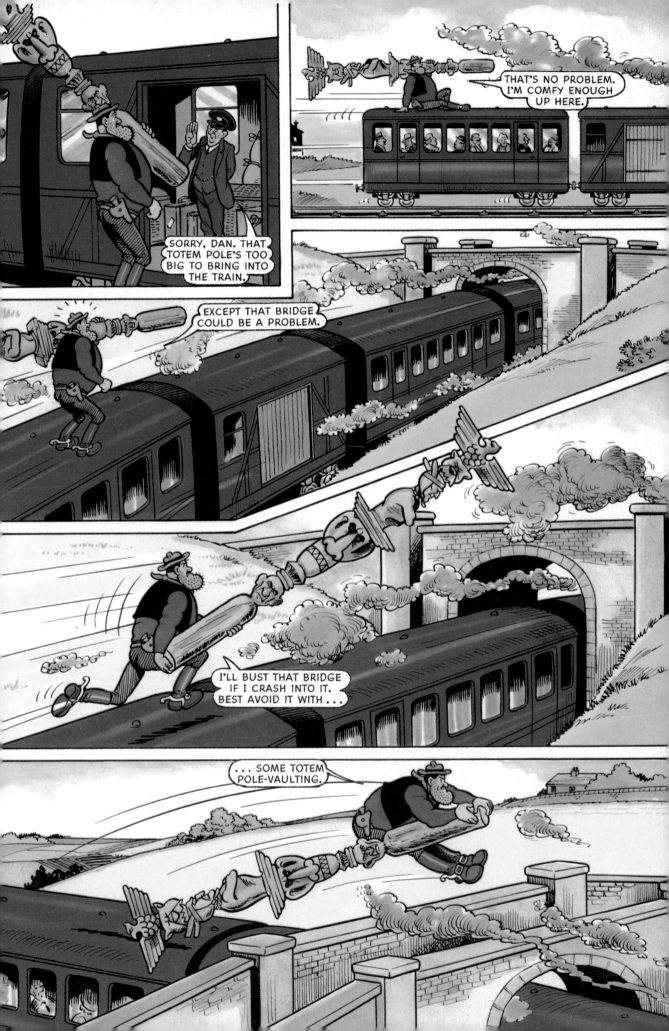

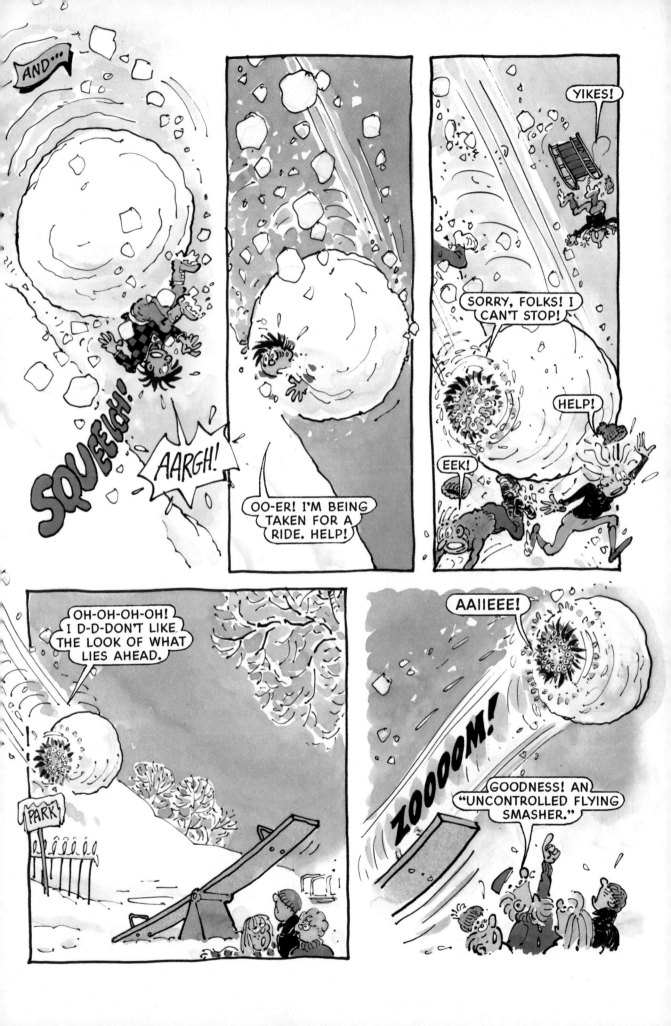

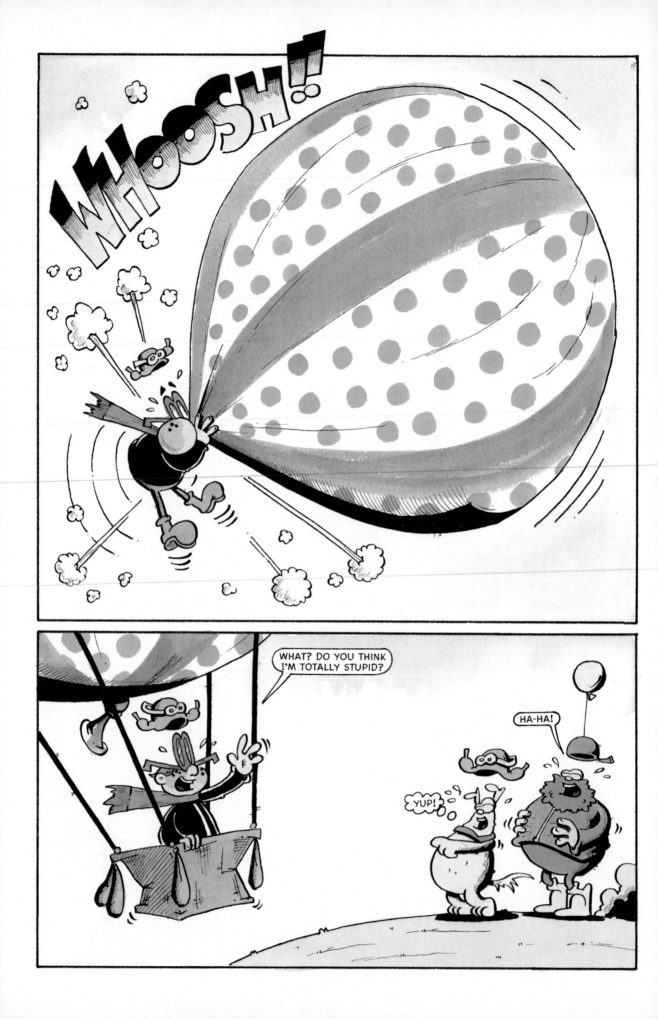

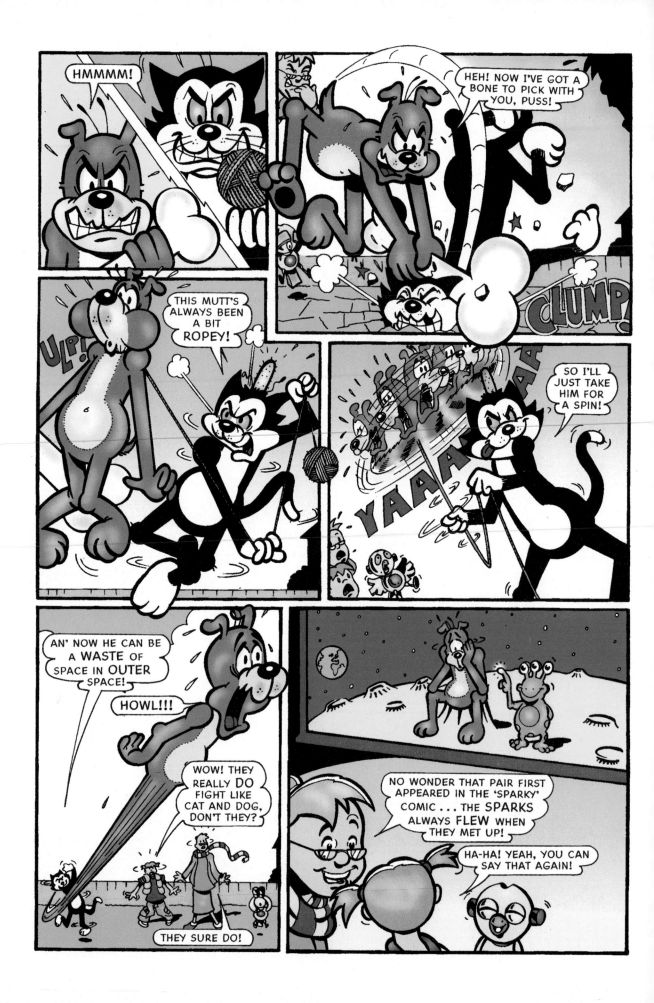

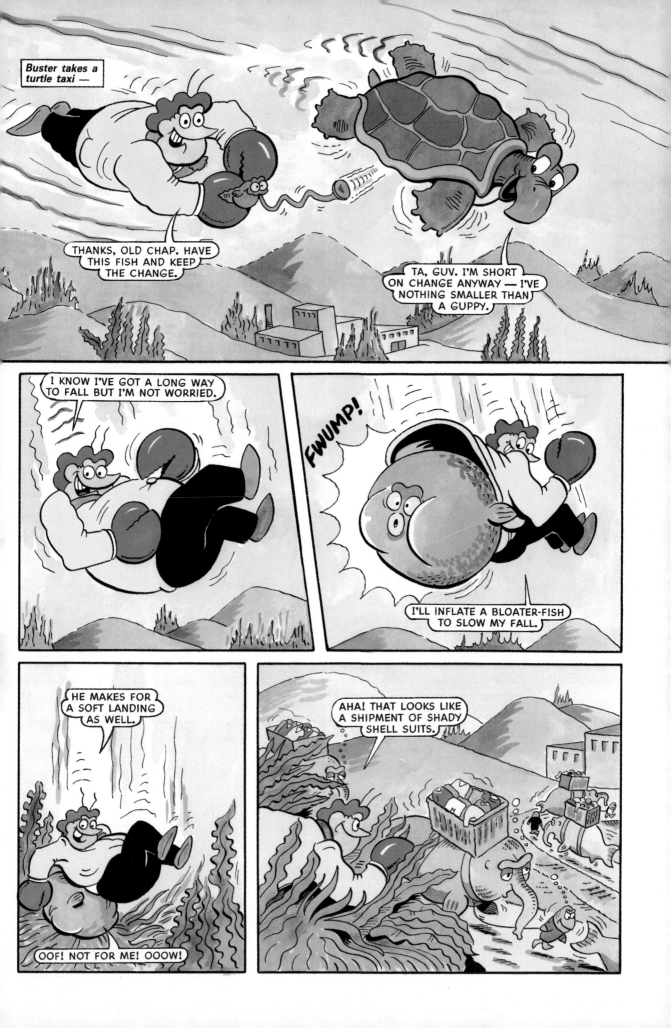

MEET THE GANG

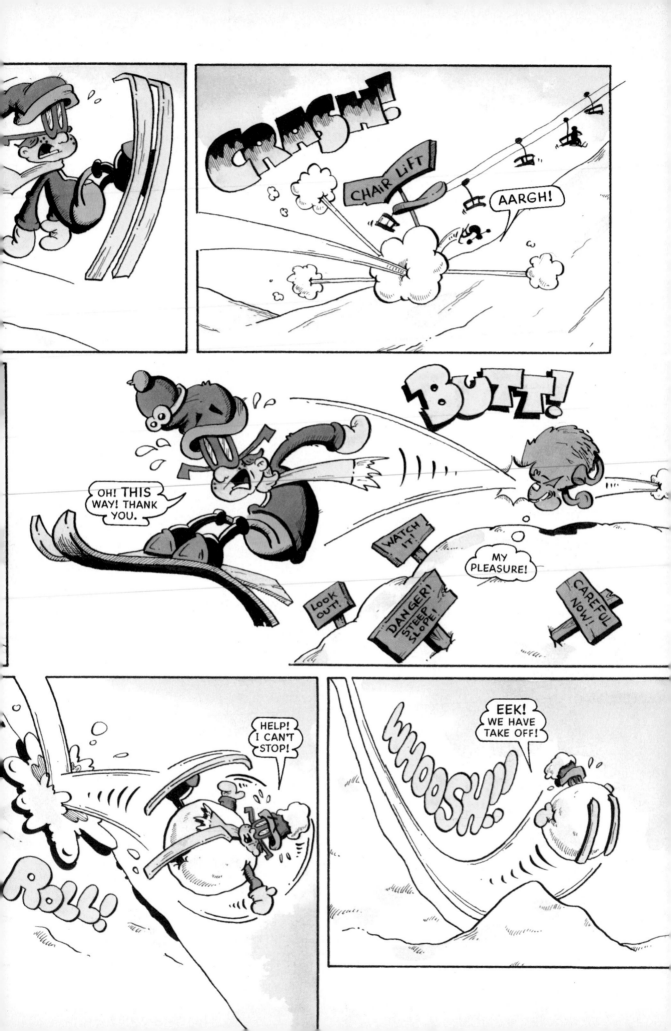

Everyone knows that Desperate Dan lives in Cactusville but he's one of the few people around able to say that he has two home towns.

The Wild West hero was created in 1937 for issue 1 of The Dandy at the comic's offices in Dundee on the east coast of Scotland. The comic has run constantly ever since with every issue being produced in Dundee.

To celebrate Dan's continued success the giant statue of Desperate Dan was unveiled on 19th July, 2001 in the High Street, Dundee by a group of local schoolchildren and . . . Dan himself who had come to see what all the fuss was about.

Visitors to Dundee can find the bronze of Dan just opposite the City Square.

THE UNVEILING

Printed and Published in Great Britain by D. C. THOMSON & CO., LTD., 185 Fleet Street, London, EC4A 2HS.
© D. C. THOMSON & CO., LTD., 2002   ISBN 085116 809 4